Lucy
and the
Sea Monster
to the Rescue

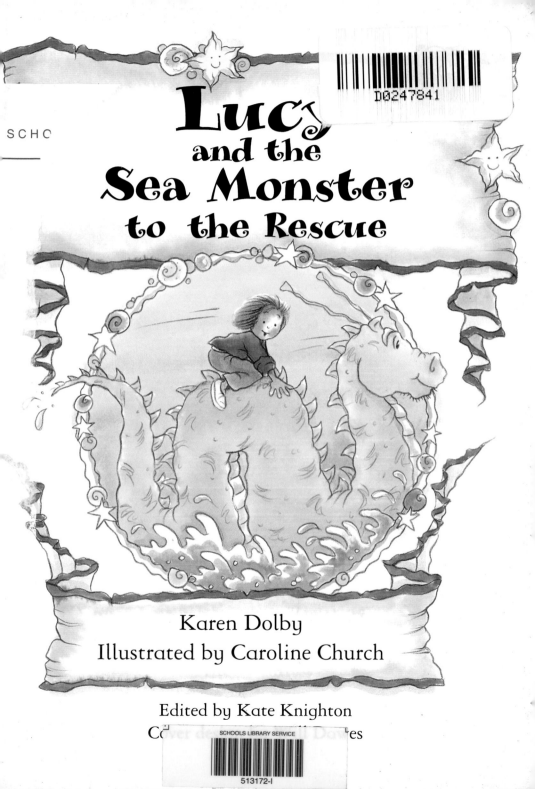

Karen Dolby

Illustrated by Caroline Church

Edited by Kate Knighton

Cover de...

Contents

The story begins

Lucy was having a boring day...

...until she looked up and saw her sea monster friend, Horace.

Keep your eyes open for clues. If you get stuck, there are answers on pages 31-32.

Message in a bottle

"Horace! Over here!" Lucy yelled, jumping up and down.

Horace and Lucy spent all morning happily splashing in the waves. Then they decided to play hide-and-seek.

As Lucy looked for a hiding place, she noticed a bottle bobbing up and down in the water. There was a note inside! She uncorked the bottle and took it out...

Help!
We're stranded on Treasure Island! Please come quickly.
Mel and Jim

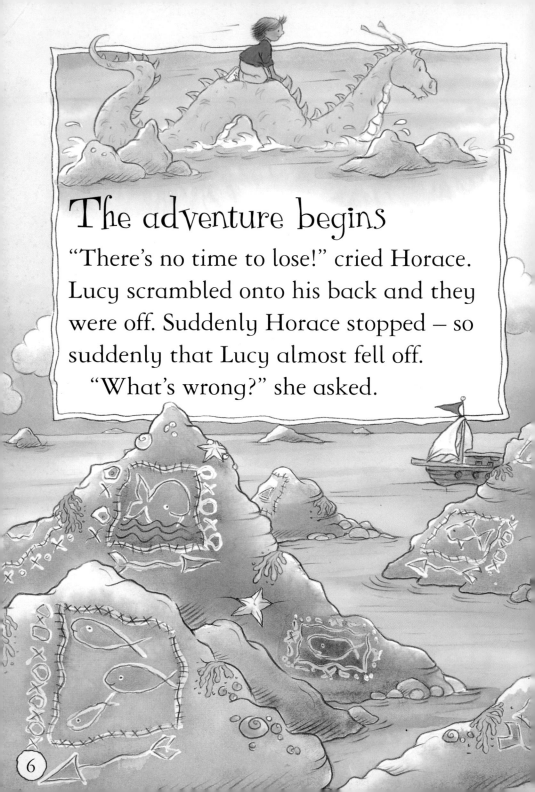

The adventure begins

"There's no time to lose!" cried Horace. Lucy scrambled onto his back and they were off. Suddenly Horace stopped – so suddenly that Lucy almost fell off.

"What's wrong?" she asked.

"I'm not sure where Treasure Island is," he admitted.

"We need help," said Lucy.

"Let's go to Neptuna, where the Merpeople live," suggested Horace. "They're sure to know the way."

Look at the signs on the rocks.
Which way should they go?

Which way?

"Oh no," cried Lucy. "We'll never find our way through all of these rocks!"

"Don't worry," said Horace. "I can see a path through the maze."

Can you find a safe way through the rocky maze?

Neptuna

Lucy gazed in wonder at Neptuna.
It was a strange and exciting place.
  "It's market day," Horace said.
Suddenly Lucy noticed the floating
stalls, piled high with shining shells,
pretty pearls and coral combs.

"Let's see if anyone knows where Treasure Island is," said Lucy.

But no one did.

"Why don't you ask Rory, our roving reporter," a merman suggested. "He knows everything. He's the one with binoculars and a notebook."

Can you see Rory?

Rory's news

"Well, the good news is that Treasure Island is easy to spot," said Rory. "There are three pointed mountains, with a tree at the top of the middle one. But it's a long, cold journey through Penguin Islands."

Lucy gulped, but there was worse to come.

"The really bad news is that there are pirates heading there too."

They all shivered. Pirates were mean and greedy. Just then, Lucy spied something that gave her a nasty shock.

What has Lucy spotted?

Penguin Islands

Lucy and Horace set off for Penguin Islands. Penguins love ice and cold, and it grew chillier and chillier the closer they got. Heavy snow began to fall.

Horace tried his best, but it was hard to see through the thick snowflakes. It was even harder to steer between the jagged ice blocks, diving penguins and huge whales barring their way.

Can you find a clear route through the icy islands?

The pirates' lair

As Horace and Lucy left Penguin Islands, the sun began to shine. They saw an island in the distance. Could it be Treasure Island?

They got a shock when they went ashore – pirates!

"Yikes! This isn't Treasure Island," whispered Horace. "This is Booty Island, the pirates' base. I can see Red Reg Rover, Short Tom Gold, Black Beard and Peg Pinafore."

Can you tell which pirate is which?

Chocolate Island

Horace and Lucy didn't wait to hear more. They slipped silently away. Horace swam low in the water and Lucy lay flat on his back, so the pirates wouldn't spot them.

They soon reached another island with candy trees and a chocolate fudge stream. The famous Chocolate Island! Lucy licked her lips hungrily.

"Let's take some sweet food and drink for Mel and Jim," said Horace.

"How will we carry it?" asked Lucy.

Can you find something to put the food and drink in?

Lucy on the lookout

They soon filled the beaker and backpack.
"Let's go," said Horace. "I think one of those islands is Treasure Island. Climb this tree and have a look. It has three pointed mountains with a tree on the middle one."

Can you spot Treasure Island?

Sea Storm

They had just set off when, without warning, a terrible storm hit them. Icy cold rain began to pour down.

"It's no good," yelled Horace above the roar of the wind and waves. "We need to find somewhere to shelter."

Can you find a safe hiding place?

A safe shelter

Safe and dry in a cave, Lucy and Horace watched lightning zigzag across the sky. A clap of thunder made Lucy jump, but she soon saw something much more scary.

What has Lucy seen?

It was the pirates' ship and it was speeding towards Treasure Island.

"Quick! We have to rescue Mel and Jim before the pirates arrive!" cried Lucy.

"Hop on my back," said Horace. "I have an idea that just might work..."

A tricky crossing

"Our only hope is to try to take a shortcut to Treasure Island," Horace explained. "But I don't like the look of it. It's not going to be easy..."

Can you find a way through? Beware of the rocks, sharks, crocodiles and lurking creatures.

To the rescue

The tricky shortcut had been worth it. They had beaten the pirates to the island. And what's more, Mel and Jim had found a treasure chest.

The pirate ship was still a long way off. "Land ahoy!" the lookout yelled, peering through his telescope. Then he let out a groan. "Bothering barnacles! We've been beaten to the loot. Let's get 'em!"

You made it. Look! We've found treasure.

28

Lucy couldn't wait to look inside the chest. But it wasn't the gold the pirates were probably hoping to find.

"It's the ancient, magical statue of Marlin!" Horace exclaimed joyfully. "It was stolen years ago from our underwater palace."

Suddenly Lucy spied the pirates' boat. "They're coming! Quick, let's go!" She cried.

Does the statue remind you of anyone?

Homeward bound

With the pirates in hot pursuit, Horace swam as fast as he dared through the sharp rocks. At last they reached clear water. But where were the pirates?

They had no need to fear. The pirates were so busy thinking about treasure, that they had run their boat aground.

Lucy smiled as they set off for home. "They won't be bothering us again."

Answers

Pages 6-7
Can you find the mermaid drawn on the rock? It is just behind Horace. The arrow shows which direction they should take.

Pages 8-9
The safe route through the maze is marked here.

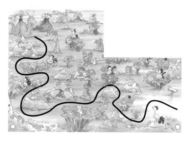

Pages 10-11
Rory is here.

Pages 12-13
Lucy has spotted a skull and crossbones pirate flag. She is worried that these are the pirates Rory just told them about.

Pages 14-15
The way through the ice is shown here.

Pages 16-17
Did you guess who each pirate was from the names?

Red Reg Rover   Black Beard

Short Tom Gold   Peg Pinafore

Pages 18-19
Here are a backpack and beaker.

Pages 20-21
Treasure Island is here.

Pages 22-23
They can hide in the cave circled below. It will protect them from the storm and it is the only one which does not have a creature lurking inside.

Pages 24-25
Lucy has seen the pirate ship sailing by.

Pages 26-27
Their route to Treasure Island is marked here.

Pages 28-29
The treasure is a gold sea monster's head. It looks a little like Horace!

This edition first published in 2008 by Usborne Publishing Ltd., Usborne House, 83-85 Saffron Hill, London EC1N 8RT, England. www.usborne.com Copyright © 2008, 2002, 1997 Usborne Publishing Ltd. The name Usborne and the devices 🔱 🎈 are Trade Marks of Usborne Publishing Ltd. All rights reserved.